Kipper tips it in.

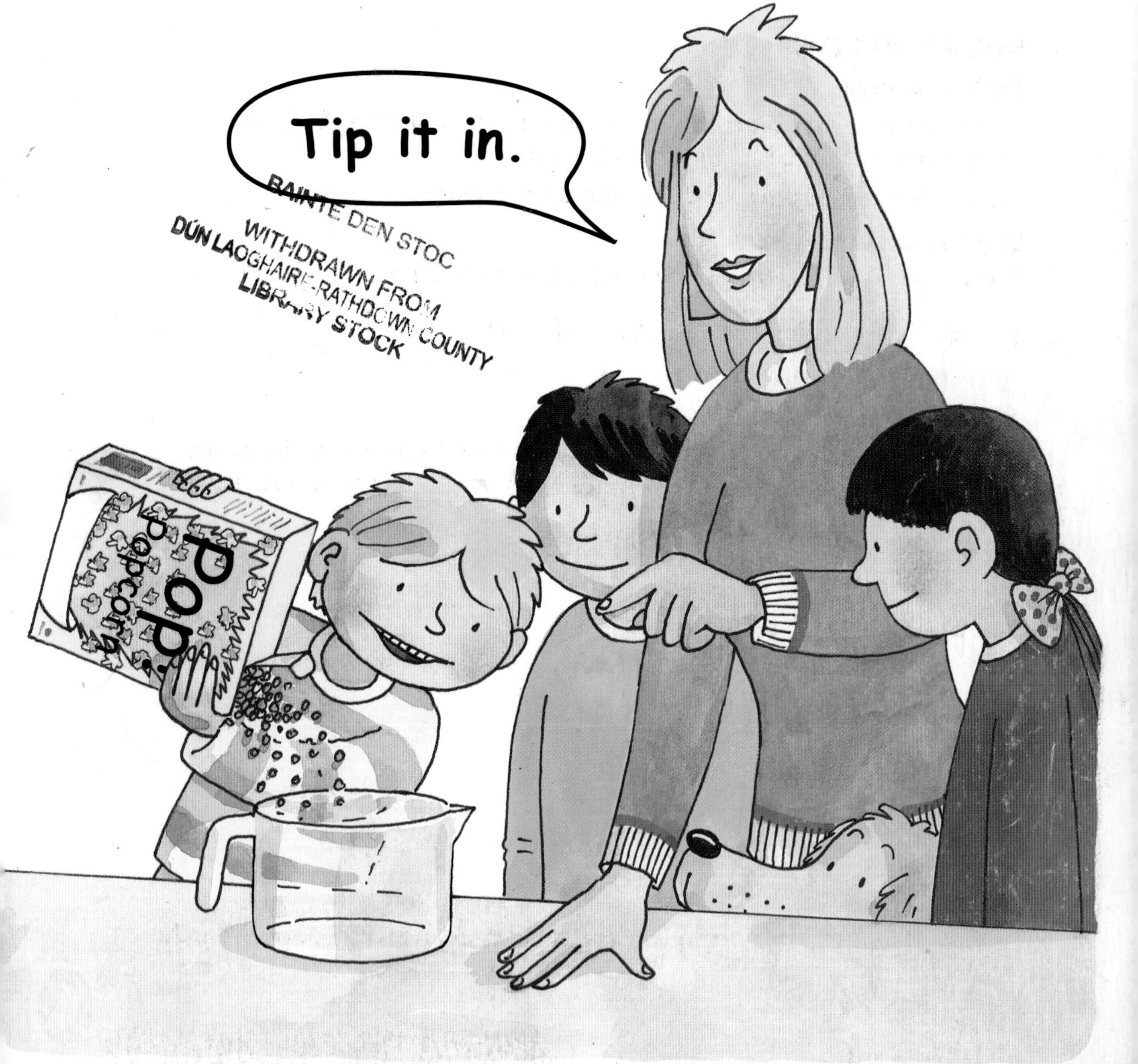
Tip it in.
Pop!
popcorn

Biff puts it in the pan.

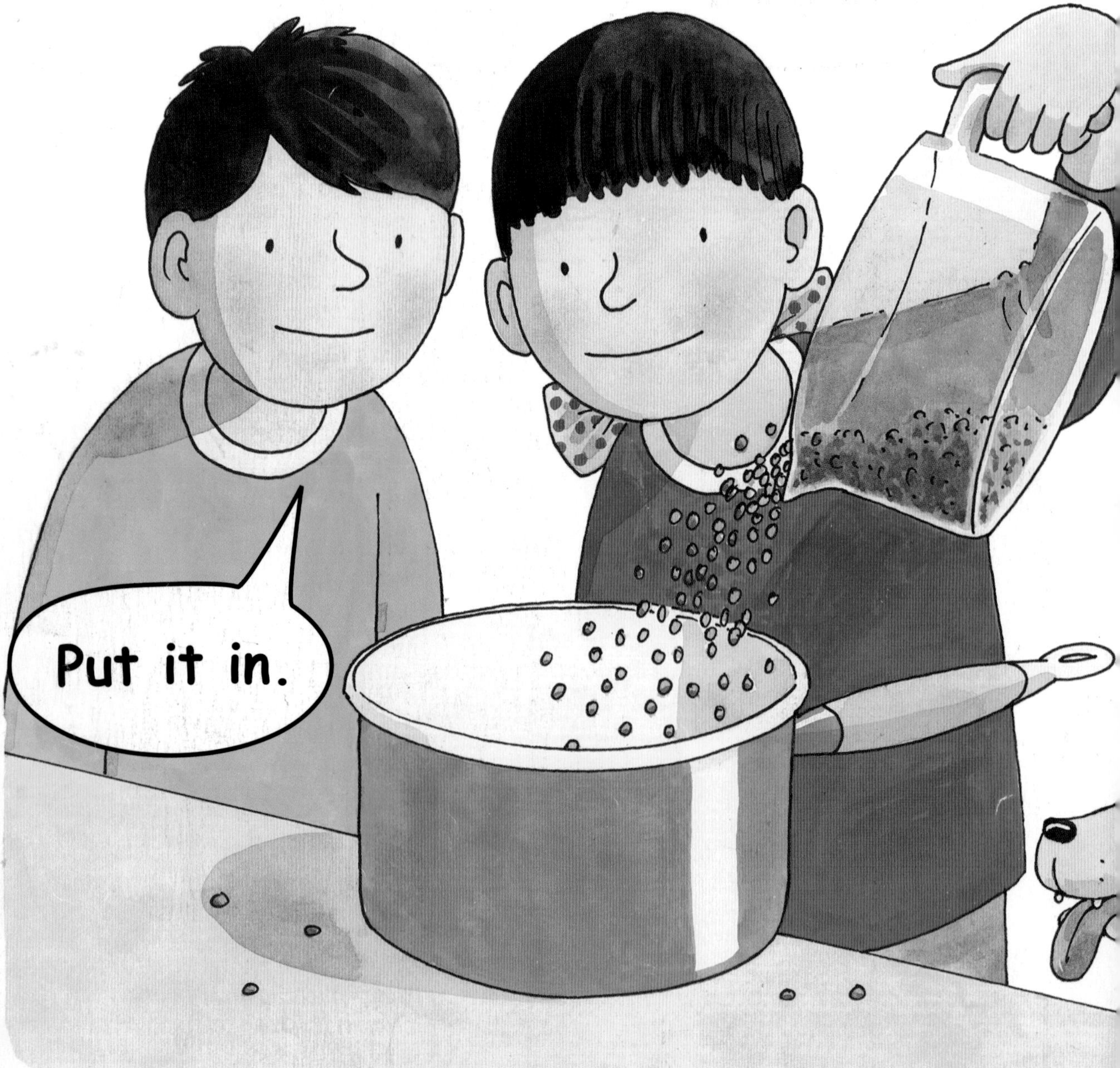

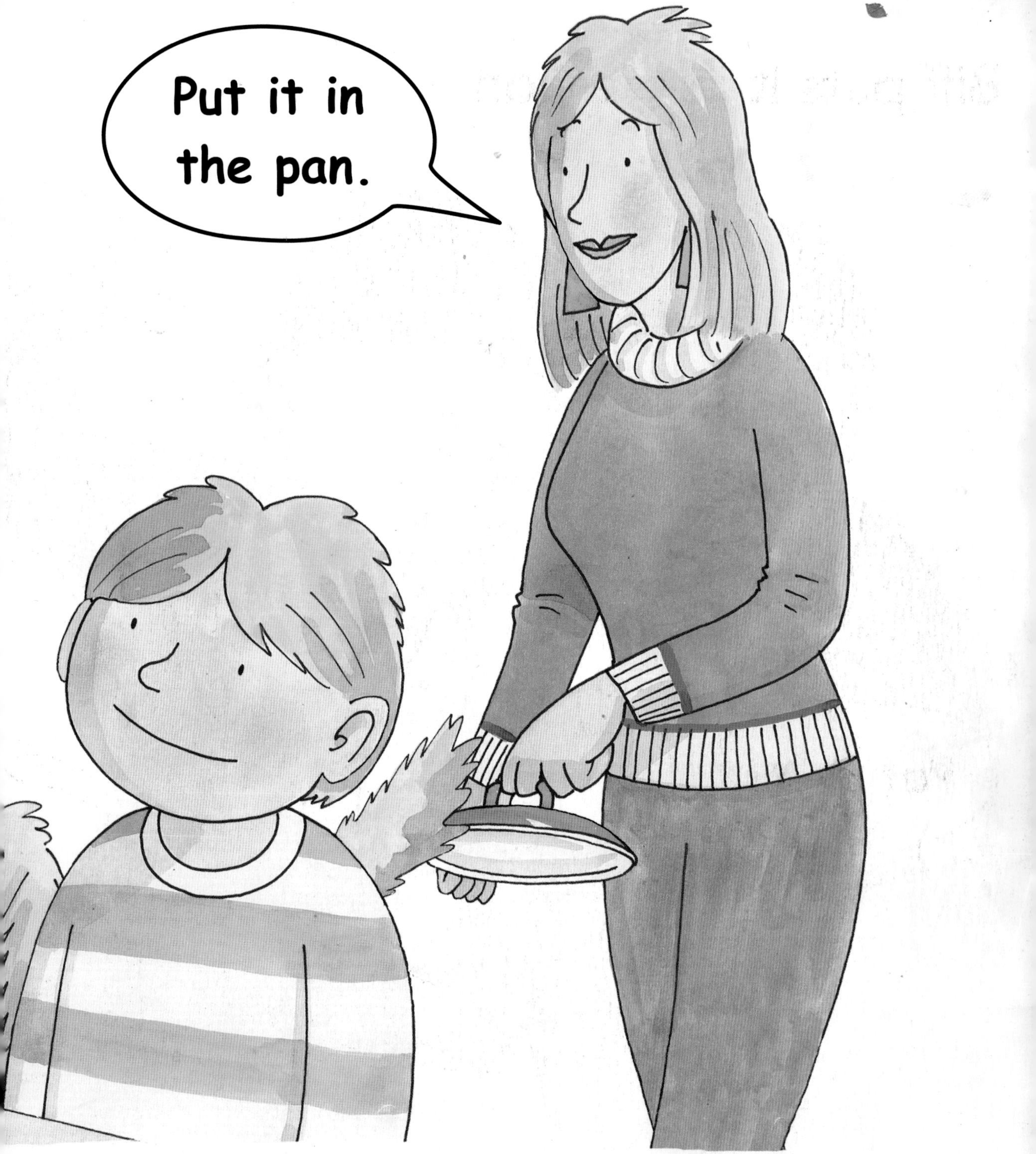
Put it in the pan.

Chip puts on the lid.

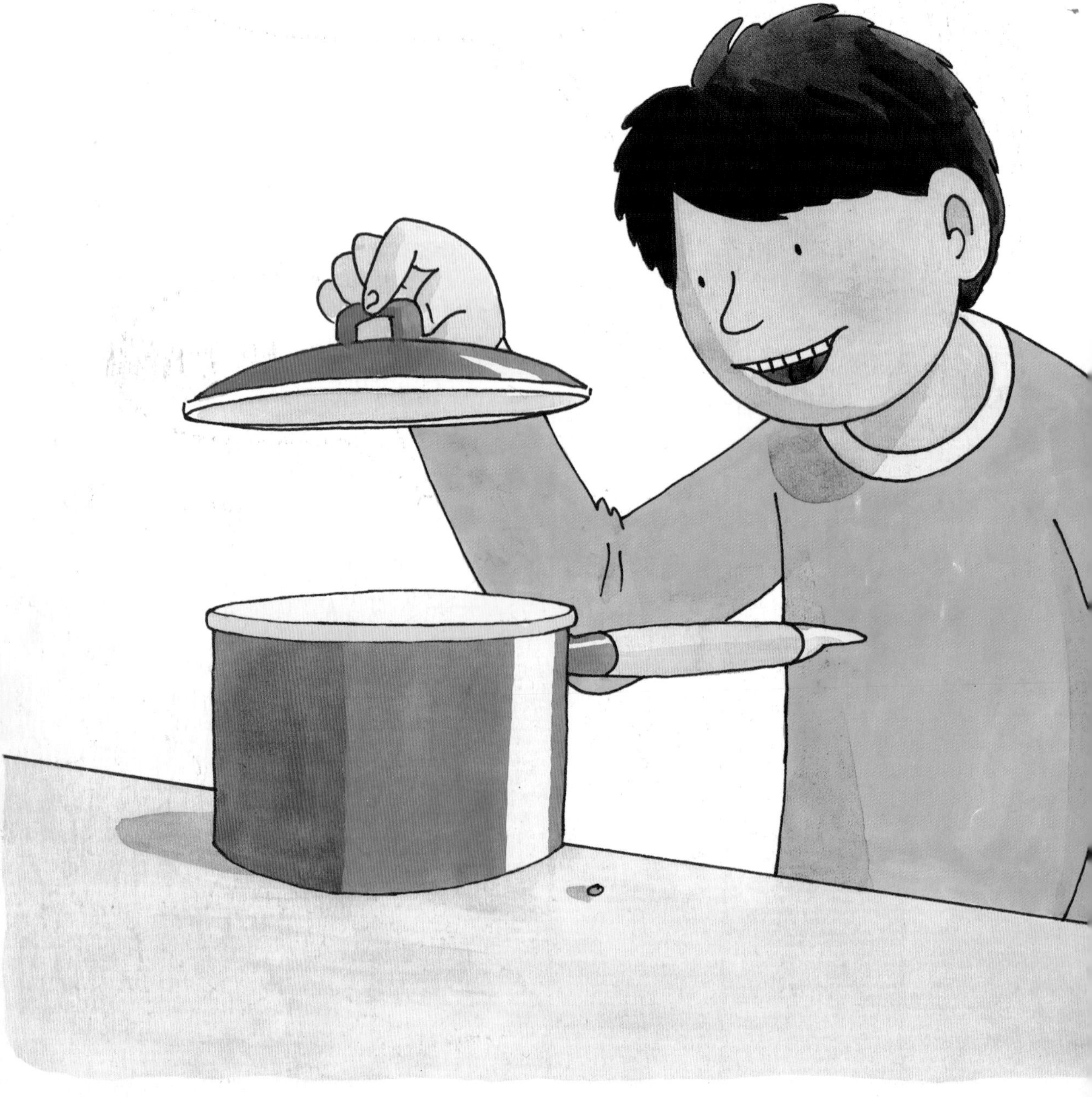

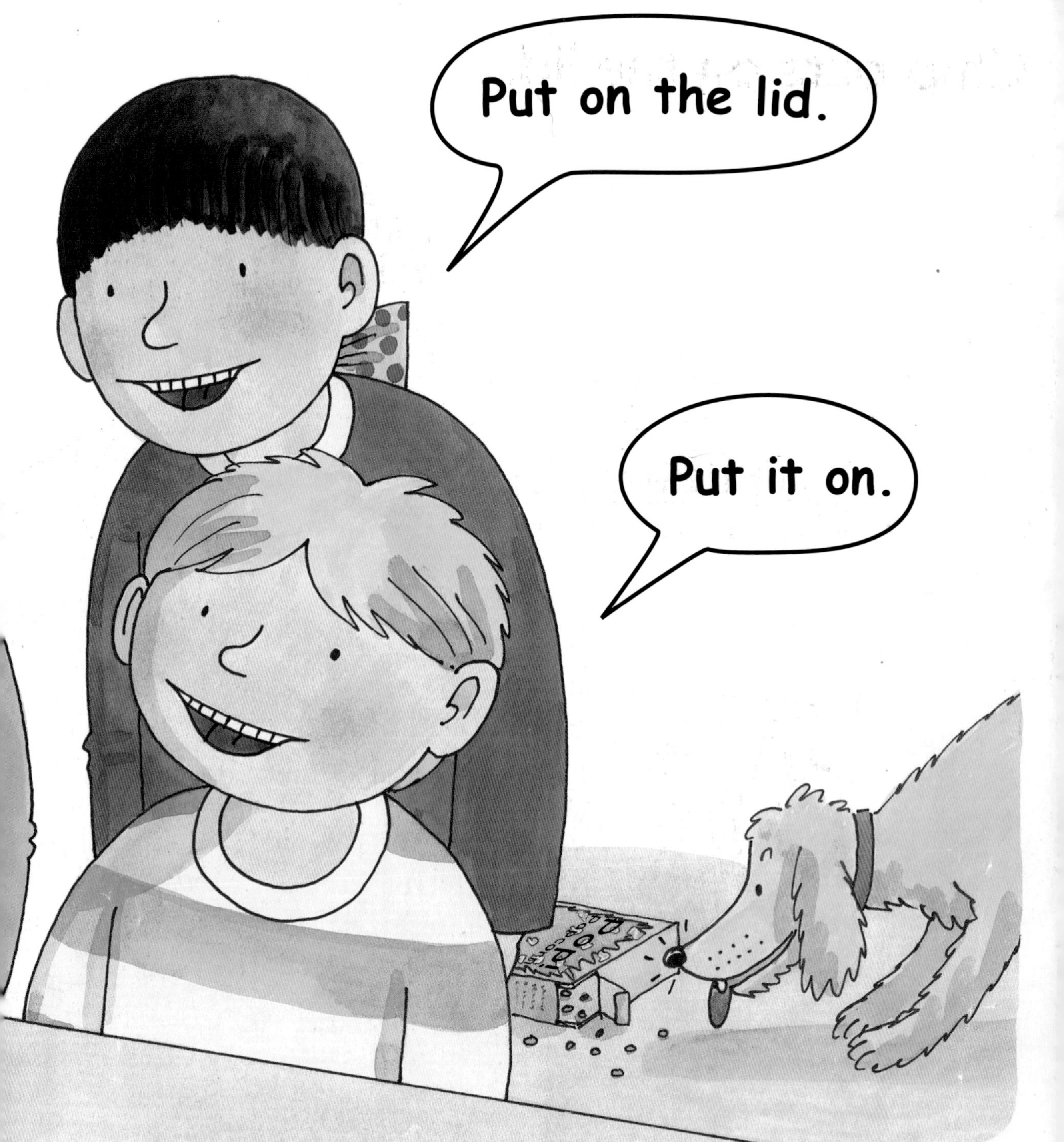
Put on the lid.
Put it on.

Mum puts the pan
on the gas.

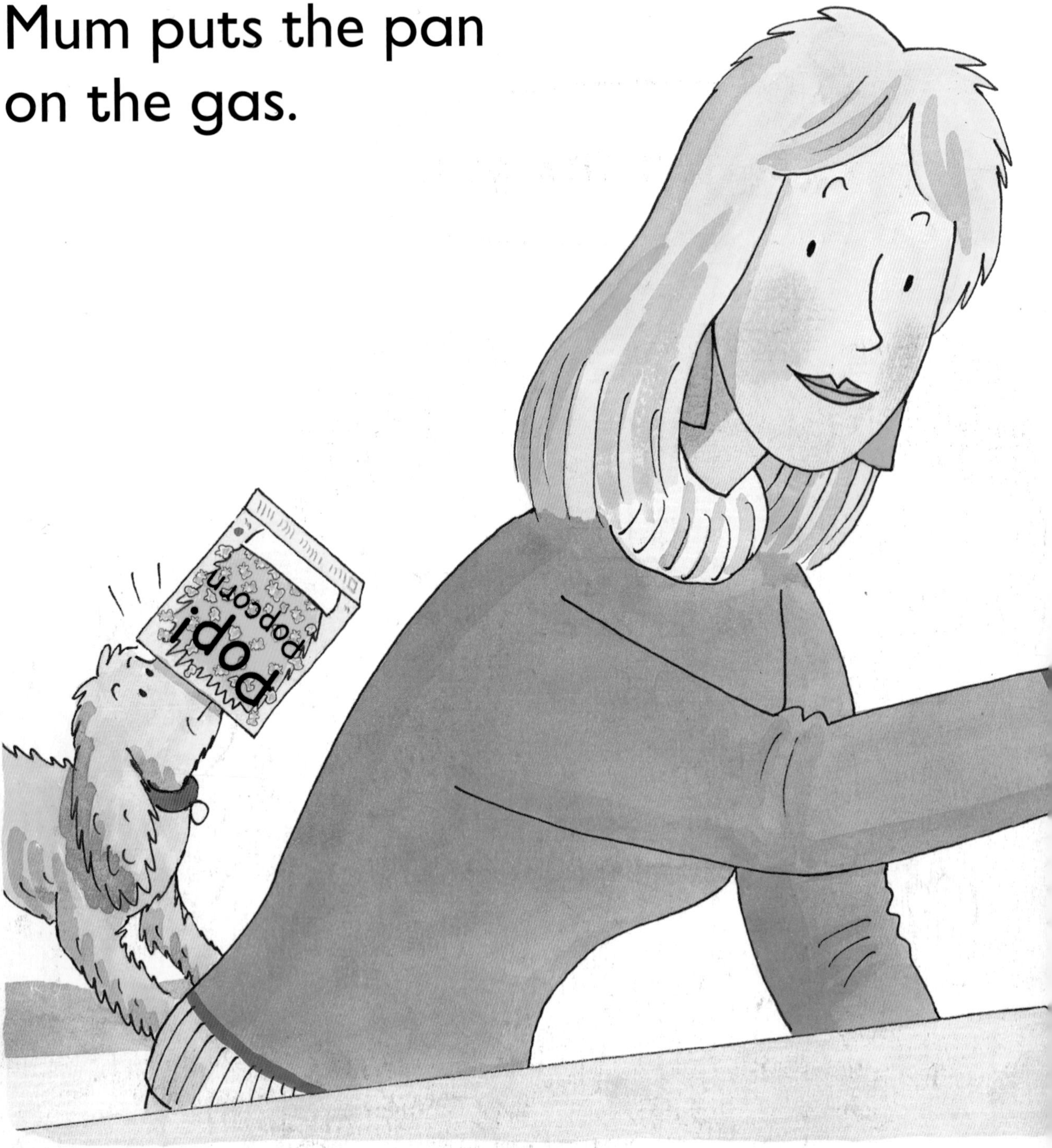

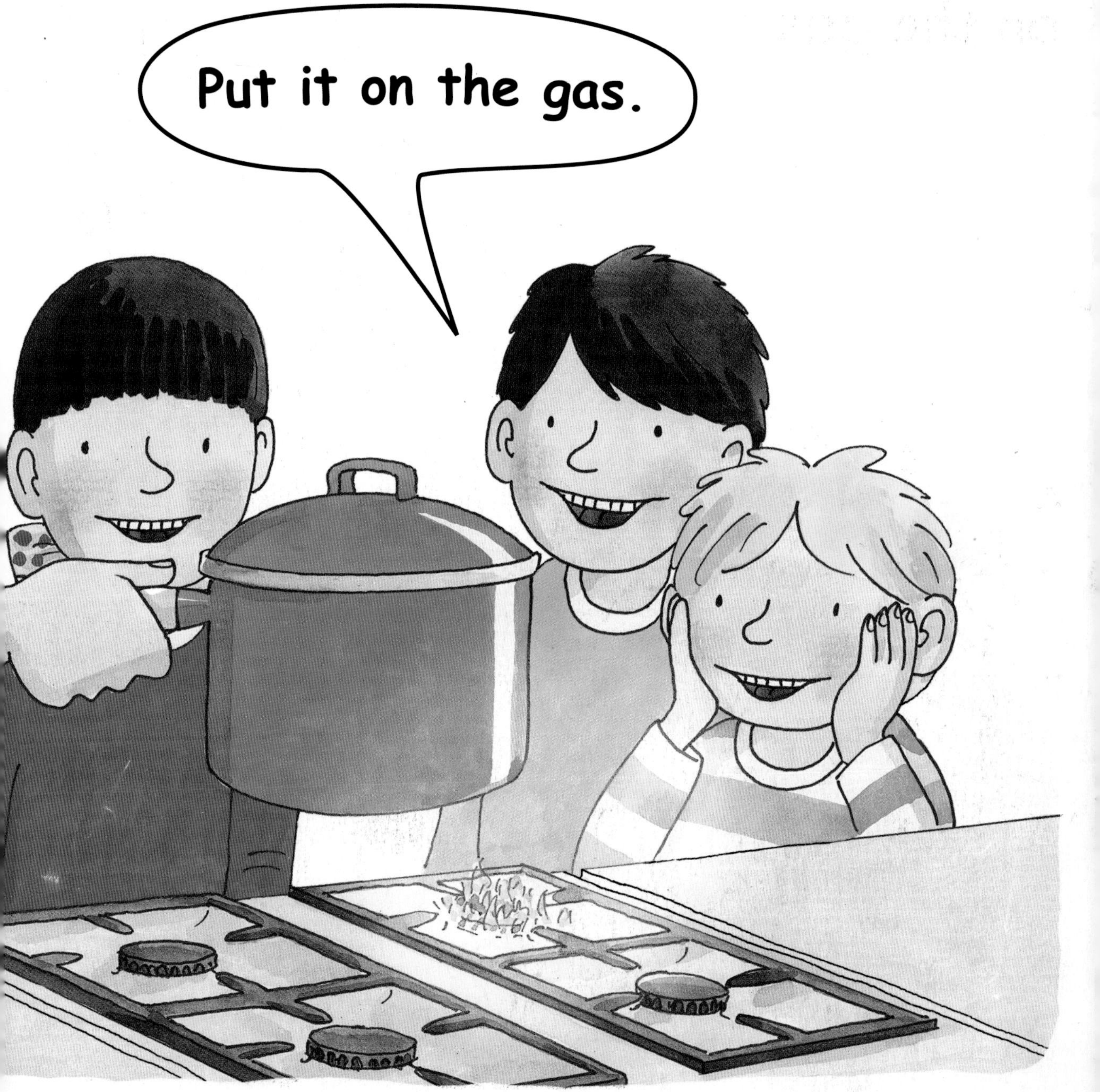
Put it on the gas.

Pop! Pop! Pop!

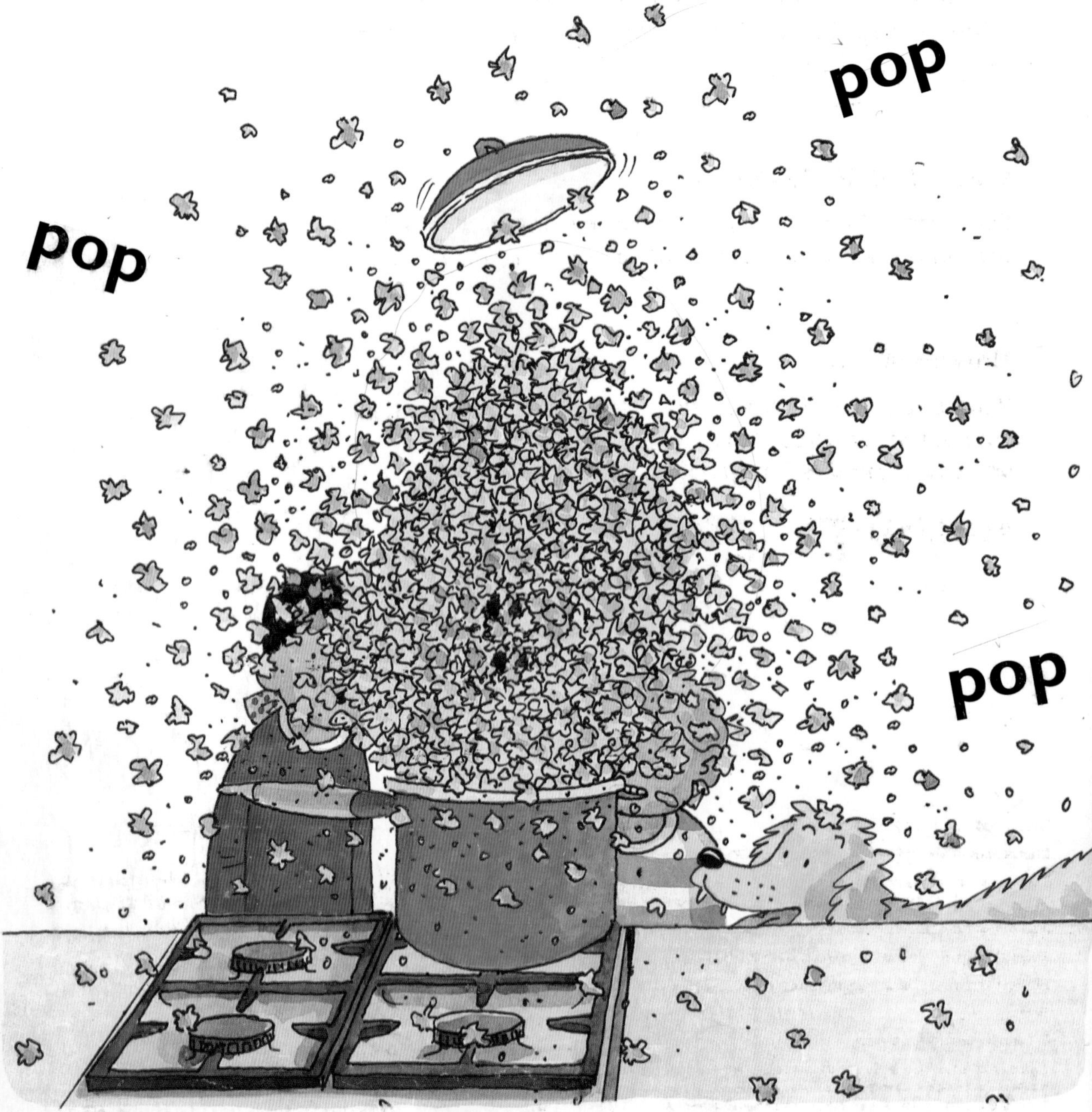